Edmung B. O'Callaghan

A Brief and True Narrative

Of the hostile conduct of the barbarous natives towards the Dutch nation

Edmung B. O'Callaghan

A Brief and True Narrative
Of the hostile conduct of the barbarous natives towards the Dutch nation

ISBN/EAN: 9783337302719

Printed in Europe, USA, Canada, Australia, Japan

Cover: Foto ©Andreas Hilbeck / pixelio.de

More available books at **www.hansebooks.com**

A

BRIEF AND TRUE

NARRATIVE

OF THE

HOSTILE CONDUCT

OF THE

BARBAROUS NATIVES

TOWARDS

The Dutch Nation.

TRANSLATED BY

E. B. O'CALLAGHAN.

ALBANY:

J. MUNSELL, 78 STATE STREET.

MDCCCLXIII.

To the Reader.

THE Paper, of which the following is a Tranſlation, is to be found in Vol. VI of the Original Dutch MSS. in the Secretary's Office, Albany, N. Y. It conſiſts of a Petition dated 31ſt October, 1655, one copy of which was addreſſed to the States General of the United Netherlands; another to the Burgomaſters and Common Council of the City of Amſterdam, and a third to the Directors of the Weſt India Company, Chamber at Amſterdam. In order to throw further light on the ſubject, a few illuſtrative Documents are added in the Appendix.

NARRATIVE.

W E Your High Mighti-
nesses and Honours Pe-
tioners, with due Reverence
and in all Humility, and so far
as our Knowledge extends, with
all Justice and Truth, repre-
sent --- That through God's
Providence and under Your
Commission and Protection,
and with the Knowledge and
Consent of the Lord Directors,
we have transported ourselves
and settled down in this Pro-

Petition from New Netherland.

New Nether-
land like Fa-
therland in
Climate, &c.
vince of *New Netherland*,---a
Country not varying from our
Fatherland in refpect of Climate and Fertility---in which,
too, we Your Petitioners and
Subjects can eafily earn a Live-
lihood; have for a long time
fupported ourfelves and could
indeed ftill further live with
apparent Hope of producing
there many and divers good
Crops and Commodities, if
we could be in any wife fe-
Hoftilities of
the Natives
towards the
Dutch.
cured, and remain protected
from the Moleftations, Vexa-
tions and Murders of the Native
Barbarians, at whofe Hands we
have fuffered many Infolencies,
in the Slaying of our Cattle

and Killing of our People, with the Particulars whereof, in paſt Times, we will not incumber Your Honours.

In order not to ſpin out a too tedious Relation nor divert Your Attention from graver and weightier Affairs, we will only ſay, in a word, that after a two years' War had been waged againſt the *Dutch* by divers barbarous *Indian* Tribes, the Lawfulneſs or Unlawfulneſs whereof we will not diſcuſs to any one's Diſparagement, a firm and irrefragable Peace was Peace conclud-ed in 1645. finally concluded, in the Year *Sixteen Hundred Five and Forty*, with the Natives afore-

Conditions
thereof.
faid, on the Conditions hereunto annexed.

Since then In-
dians kill many
Cattle and mur-
der feveral Per-
fons.
Thofe Indian Nations have,
fince that time, without any
caufe as far as we know, not
only flain and killed many
Animals, fuch as Cows, Horfes
and Hogs, your Subjects' property, but even cruelly murdered ten Perfons, *videlicet :*
Firft, *Symon Walingen* in the
fecond Year after the Peace
had been concluded ; the Wife
of *Jan Pieterfen* on *Long Ifland* in the year *Sixteen Hundred One and Fifty ;* in the
Year *Sixteen Hundred and
Fifty-two,* four Perfons on this
Ifland of *Manhattan ;* again,

one Year after that, three People on *Staten Ifland*, and laft
Year *Jochim Pieterfen Kuyter*
in his own Houfe.

The Supreme Government
of this Province hath demanded
the Murderers, but thefe have
always been refufed; certes,
have never been forthcoming;
and for the fake of Peace and
out of confideration for the
good and advantage of the
Country and its People, the
Government hath without any
Manifeftation of Hoftility or
Revenge, winked at this Infraction of the Peace.

Now, it hath further come
to pafs, that on the *fifteenth* of

The Murderers
demanded, but
not given up.

Infraction of
the Peace
winked at.

Director General goes to reduce the Swedes at the South River. .
the laft month, *September*--- after the *Honourable* the Director General had, purfuant to Your Honours' Orders and Defpatches, taken his Departure, with the few Soldiers belonging to this Province, for the *South River* of *New Netherland*, for the purpofe of refenting the Affronts and Infults fuffered from the *Swedes*, and of reducing that River again under this Province---(the Blefling of God on which

A large body of Savages land at New Amfterdam.
Expedition we moft gratefully acknowledge)---*fourteen* Days after the *Honble* Director's Departure, very early in the Morning,. nigh this City of

New Amſterdam, arrived *ſixty-four* Canoes full of *Indians*, who before ſcarcely anyone was yet riſen ſcattered themſelves throughout this City, and during the following Day, in many Houſes and to divers Burghers offered numerous Inſults, all which to particularize would draw this humble Petition to too great a length.

Their inſolent behaviour.

Thereupon their *Sackimas*, or Chiefs, being ſummoned before the Council, gave very fair Words, and promiſed to depart before the Evening. They remained, neverthelefs, with what Intent God the Lord only knows.

Their Sackimas called before the Council and promiſe to depart.

Meanwhile, the honeſt Burgh-

ers, irritated at the Insults suf-
fered throughout that Day, very
prudently and through fear of
further Mischief, doubled the
Guards during the following
Night, by command of the remaining Councillors and other
Officers.   About eight o'clock,
one *Paulus Leendertsen* was,
according to his Declaration,
threatened with an Axe, and
the late Fiscal *Van Dyck* was
wounded with an Arrow within this City.   Thereupon great
Uproar and Tumult arose;
some of the Burghers got into
Conflict with the *Indians*, and
some, though few, were killed
on both Sides.   Shortly after-

The Guards doubled.

Mr. Leendert-sen threatened and the late Fiscal wounded.

Consequent conflict; some killed.

wards and throughout the whole of the following Night, thofe Indian Tribes laid wafte the Settlements by a terrible Fire and Maffacre to fuch an extent that, in three Days, full *Fifty* Chriftians were murdered and put to Death ; over *One Hundred*, moftly Women and Children, were captivated, whereof *Sixty* to *Seventy* were afterwards ranfomed at a great Expenfe, the Balance ftill remaining in their Hands ; *Twenty-eight* Bouweries and a number of Plantations were burnt with full *Twelve* to *Fifteen Hundred* Skepels of Grain ; and *Five* to *Six Hundred* head of Cattle

Terrible devaftation of the furrounding fettlements.

Numbers murdered and 100 captivated.

Farms laid wafte and crops deftroyed.

either killed or ſtill in poſſeſſion of the Barbarians. Truly, *Right Honorable,* Your Subjects and humble Petitioners have at the hands of theſe Barbarous

Eſtimated loſs.

Savages, ſuffered a loſs of twice *One Hundred Thouſand* Guilders; and over *Three Hundred* Souls, excluſive of thoſe who have been ſlain or led away into Captivity, are diſpoſſeſſed of their Properties and not left wherewithall to provide Food and Raiment either for themſelves or their Families, have

Impoveriſhed condition of New Netherland.

now become a Burthen to the Burghers of this City alone. Finally, the Country in general is ſo impoveriſhed that it will not for Years be brought back to the flouriſhing Condition in which it was *Six* ſhort Weeks ago.

When to all this is ſuper-added the Fear which poſſeſſes, and not without reaſon, the majority of the Inhabitants of being again as ſuddenly ſur-prized, in caſe no Remedy be employed againſt ſo general a Maſſacre and ſo vaſt a Loſs, it cauſes them and many others to be cautious, and afraid of again returning to the *Flat-Land.* Indeed, this is an Im-poſſibility to them, unleſs others lend them a helping Hand. From all which, then, in Con-

Inhabitants un-willing to re-turn to their Bouweries.

clufion, nothing is to be ex-
pected through want of Culti-
vation of the Soil and Failure
of Crops, but Poverty, Want,
Famine, and the final and
utter Ruin of the Country.

Ruin of the Country imminent.

We, Your Honours' Sub-
jects and humble Petitioners,
lay this fad and forrowful Condition of ourfelves and of the
Country before you, in all
Reverence and Humility, im-
ploring at the fame time
Counfel and Affiftance how to
act towards thofe Barbarous
Tribes in return for thefe and
other Murders, Affronts and
ferious Loffes. Moft unwilling
fhould we be, without your

Affiftance and advice afked for.

Honours' previous Knowledge, Counſel and Help, to initiate an open War, which it is naturally impoſſible for us to wage and bring to a deſirable Iſſue, unleſs next to God's Aſſiſtance, we obtain Help and Aid from our beloved Fatherland.

Unable to wage war unleſs aided.

All which being duly conſidered by us, together with the preſent Inability of the *Honble* Directors of the Incorporated Weſt India Company to ſend us ſuch and ſo ſpeedy Succour as the Neceſſity and Circumſtances of the Country in general demand, we deem it expedient, in order to avoid

Send an agent to the Weſt India Company;

all Exceptions and Charges of Neglect, in not having given Information to the Supreme Government, to addreſs this our humble Supplication firſt and foremoſt to Your Honours (of the Company) and in addition, but with your previous Knowledge and Approbation, to their High Mightineſſes and the Moſt Worſhipful the Regents of the City Amſterdam, or wherever elſe Your Honours will direct *Cornelis Jacobſen Steenwyck,* our Agent.

To the States General, and to the Burgomaſters of Amſterdam.

The Succour wherewith we hope, with God's merciful Help and Aſſiſtance, to reduce the aforeſaid Barbarous Tribes to

to Obedience, and to poffefs the
Land again in Peace and without Fear, fhould, with Submif-
fion to your Honours' better
Judgment, confift of *Three* or Number of fol-
diers required;
their arms.
Four Thoufand (a) good Soldiers,
armed one-half with Match-
locks, one-half with Wheel-
locks (*Snaphance*) of *three* and
one-half feet Barrel, carrying
Sixteen Bullets to the Pound
and no more, who after the
Work is done would be willing
to fettle in the Country for the
increafe of its Population.   A
Supply to the amount of *Thirty*
or *Forty Thoufand* Guilders, in

(a) The figures are 3 or 400 in another draft of the petition.

fuitable Commodities for the Clothing and Support of the Military, is moſt urgently required, together with ſome neceſſary Ammunition according to the annexed Liſt.

Right Honourable Lords and Patroons:

We Your Honours' Subjects and Petitioners humbly ſupplicate you to take this our humble Remonſtrance and Supplication into your ſerious Confideration, and ſo to favor us, that we may ſpeedily receive good Advice and Aſſiſtance before greater Miſchiefs overtake your Subjects either here or on the reduced *South River.* Which doing you will obligate us, and all other your Honours' Subjects, to pray conftantly for your Honours' Profperity, and to remain, Right Honourable, Prudent and Honourable Lords,

Your Honours'

Humble Servants.

APPENDIX.

Treaty of Sixteen Hundred and Forty-five.

THIS day, the *Thirtieth* of *Auguſt*, 1645, before the Director and Council in preſence of the entire Commonalty, appeared in Fort *Amſterdam* theſe *Sackemakers* or Indian Chiefs, both for themſelves and acting on the behalf of the circumjacent Chiefs, *To-wit :*

Oratany Chief of *Achkinckeſhacky* ; *Seſekemus* and *William*, Chiefs of *Tappaen* and *Rechgawawanck* ; *Pacham*, *Pennekeck*, who were here yeſterday and left Power with the former ; reſponding alſo for thoſe of *Onany* and their Neighbours ; *Mayauwetinnemin* for thoſe of *Marech-*

kawick, *Nayeck* and their Neighbours; together with *Aepjen*, in perſon, ſpeaking for the *Wappinex*, *Wiquacſkeckx*, *Sint-ſings* and *Kichtawangs*;

I. They agree to and conclude a firm, irrefragable Peace with us, which they have promiſed, and do promiſe to hold faſt and nevermore to break.

II. If it come to paſs, which God forbid, that any Difficulty ſhould ariſe between us and them, no War ſhall be commenced on that Account, but they ſhall apply to our *Governour* and we to their *Sackemakers*, and if any one be killed or murdered, Juſtice ſhall be immediately done to the Murderer, and we ſhall live henceforth in all Friendſhip together.

III. They ſhall not come armed near any Chriſtians' Houſes on this Iſland of *Manhatan*, and we will not approach theirs with Guns, unleſs accompanied by an Indian to give them Warning.

IV. And whereas they have still an Englifh Maiden with them, whom they have promifed to convey to the Englifh at *Stamford;* this they likewife promife to do, and if fhe be not conveyed thither, they promife to bring her here and we will pay them the Ranfom which the Englifh have promifed for her.

All that is above written we promife fhall be ftrictly obferved throughout the whole of *New Netherland.*

Thus done in the Fort, under the *Blue Sky,* before the Council of *New Netherland* and the intire Commonalty thereunto convoked, in Prefence of the Mohawk Ambaffadors who were invited to attend as Mediators at this Negotiation of Peace, and *Claes Antonifen* their Interpreter and Co-Mediator herein. Dated as above. The Original was figned with

The mark of SISIADEGO.

The mark of CLAES NOORMAN.

The mark of ORATANIM.

The mark of Auronge.

The mark of Sesekemus.

The mark of William of Tappaen.

William Kieft.

La Montagne.

The mark of Jacob Stoffelsen.

John Onderhil.

Francis Douthey.

Go. Bacxter.

Richard Smith.

Gysbert Opdyc.

The mark of Aepje Sachem of the Mahikanders.

Jan Eversen Bout.

Oloff Stevensen.

Cornelis Vander Hoykens.

The mark of Cornelis Tonissen.

Lower ftood:

To my knowledge,

(Signed) Cornelis Van Tienhouen,

Secretary.

Dutch Inhabitants of Gravefend to the Director and Council.

Honourable, wife, prudent and difcreet Sirs,
The Director General and
Council of New Netherland,
Health.

Gravefend, Sept. 8, 1655.

Great and Refpectful Lords!

WE hear here dayly ftrange and uncouth Reports from Heemfted, Newtown and other places, that the Savages intend to root out the Dutch among the Englifh, demanding from the Englifh at Gravefend, that they will feparate themfelves from us, to efcape the danger of lofing, with us, their Lives and Property. They read us yefterday evening, when all were under arms, a Letter to the fame purpofe, of which we here include a copy, with many different reports, too long to be inferted here, all have a bearing to induce us to depart from here, as was propofed to us by Tilton and the Magiftrate, it being the fafeft way for us, to preferve our Lives and Property to feparate ourfelves from them, and to depart to the Manhattans, by which means the Englifh too might be faved, as they pretended. But if we were unwilling to depart, that then neverthelefs they would leave nothing untried to fave us. A poor Confolation indeed, as it appears to us if the Indians approach in confiderable numbers. It is further faid, that the Indians from the North, and the adjacent places, were making great preparations to execute their projeft, fo that they are urgently exhorting us to depart and fave our Lives as fpeedily as it is poffible.

By thefe ftrong perfuafions we are indeed perplexed and confounded, not knowing what to do or to aft, to whom to addrefs ourfelves, except to God Almighty and your Honours, who, we are confident, are willing in this dire neceffity to affift us with your Wifdom and Power, for the Water has already nearly reached our Lips. If we leave this fpot, then Long Ifland no longer has Dutch people for inhabitants. Whereupon we prefume, it well deferves the Attention of your Honours to confider what our Situation requires, although we are unable to difcover what to do in this perilous Situation. We are every day on the alert on foot and on horfeback, to obtain one another's opinion from which your Honours may prefume what Fate is threatening us.

Yefterday Tilton and the Sheriff of Newtown arrived here, to-day they return together from here. If your Hon. deemed it advifable to fave us and Long Ifland, a fmall force would be fully adequate to effect this Purpofe. But, if your Honours did prefer to fee our arrival at the Fort, our hands and feet are unable to provide for the fafety of our wives and children, not even to procure them Victuals. In that cafe it would be indifpenfable to fend a well armed Veffel towards Anthony Janfen's, with fuch a quantity of Provifions as may be deemed proper. But we truft our fituation to your Wifdom and Prudence, confident that you will refolve what is beft and defirable, and we expect your Advice and Orders, agreeably to which we fhall regulate our conduct. We are and remain your Honours Subjects,

JACOBUS VAN CORLER.
JAN THOMASSEN.
HUYBERT JANSEN HOOCK.
JACOB HELLEKAS.
LUYCAS VANDER LIPHORST.
BARENT BALTES.

† mark of HENDRICK CORNELISSEN.
( ) mark of JAN JACOBSEN.
C mark of WILLAM WILLEMSEN.
‡ mark of CORNELIS BEECKEMAN.

Mr. Thomas Wheeler to the People of Gravefend, L. I.

Weft Chefter, 27 Sept., 1655.

RESPECTED friends—After my refpects prefented unto you. I am fenfible of your feares; and it is not without grounds: I feare to ufe the beft means, as is in my power. I fhall not be wanting in mee to you for your prefervation, to fpeake with the Indians; wee know not how, the Bearer thereof can further informe you, but if you fend a meffenger about Saterday with your minde, I thincke our Saggamaker will be hear, but if you do not, my true endeavor fhall be ufed for your Safetye and and my weake advife to you at prefent, if you intend your prefervation and alfoe the Dutch, that are amongft, if they meane to fave theyre Lives, there muft be meanes ufed for them, to retourne to their own contremen for fafe guard; for this I fully underſtand, that the Indians will pick them out of every Engliſh towne upon the Iſland and in New England. It is a trouble to our Saggamackers, that there is ſo many Dutch among you, for feare they ſhould wrong you in killing of them. Soe deſiring the Lord to protect you I reſt

THOS. WHELER.

The Indians intend no wrong to the Engliſh, if they aſſiſt not the Dutch with men or proviſion.

Affidavit as to the Hoſtility of the Indians.

JOSEPH Safford, Thomas Read, reſiding near Meſpath's kill, declare, that they were informed this day by Joſeph Fowler, Goodman Beets, Samuel Tow, and his ſon-in-law William Read, that ſome of the Inhabitants of Gravefend had been at Weſtcheſter, and that there the Sachemakers of the Savages had been at Lieutenant Wheeler, and that they intended to send to the English Villages on Long Island, that these should deliver in their hands Tomas Nuton and Harry Nuton and Edward Jesop, because they in that night, when the Savages committed so much mischief, assisted the Dutch in the Fort. Further, that the Savages prohibited the English to bring any provisions whatever to the Manhattans, or any fire wood, or assist them with any sort of victuals; and in case the English assisted the Dutch with fire wood or any kind of victuals, that then they would burn their hamlets and houses. They declared that this was true, and were willing to confirm it with their oath.

Joseph Safford.

The mark of Thomas Read.

Lower stood:

This was written in the presence of the Hon. La Montagne, and the Hon. Burgomaster Allard Antony, in whose prefence the witneffes took their oaths in the hands of the Attorney General.

LA MONTAGNE.

ALLARD ATHONY.

8 September, 1655.

Opinion of Director Stuyvefant.

WE concur in the general Opinion that the Indians had, on their firft Arrival, no other intention than to wage War againft the Savages on the eaft End of Long Ifland. We have come to this Conclufion from various Reafons too long to be detailed here; and that a culpable want of Vigilance, and a too hafty Rafhnefs on the part of a few hot-headed Spirits, had diverted the Indians and been the caufe of the dreadful Confequences and enormous Loffes.

Opinion of Councillor La Montagne.

...... IT muſt be firſt aſcertained whe-
ther the Indians were the firſt
Aggreſſors or not. This muſt
be determined from their previous Action,
for granting that they did not intend any
Harm in their Proceeding, yet having
excited a reaſonable Suſpicion, and occa-
ſioned this Conflict, they will always be
deemed the Inſtigators and Aggreſſors,
and therefore the *Cauſa movens* thereof.

And *firſt :* Was not their unſeaſonable,
unannounced and unauthorized collecting
here of *Nineteen hundred* Savages, *Eight
hundred* of whom had already landed, to
make an attack on *Fifty* or *Sixty*, contrary to their uſual Cuſtoms, ſufficient to
create a Suſpicion of an evil Intent? and
did not the intollerable Inſolencies which
they committed in breaking into Mr.
Allerton's Houſe, and beating ſome Burghers in their own Houſes, increaſe that

Sufpicion afterwards? Did not their remaining here, contrary to their Promife, and the Murder which they fought to commit, after the fetting of the Watch, on Captain *Paulus Leendertfen,* afford fufficient Grounds for concluding an evil Intention on their part? And were not all the Burghers, who were to be muftered in the Fort for its Security, and being there (fince they were not called out to guard the Fort only but to protect the intire Place), were they not in duty bound to fuccour any Burgher who cried out, *Murder! Help!* And coming there, and finding the Burgher wounded in the Breaft by an Arrow, were they not bound to run to the Indians for the purpofe of examining their Faces, and when they found them with Arms and Guns, were they not juftified in making a ftand againft them? . . . . . .

Before the Attack, they had murdered, in the North, *Ten* of our People at dif-

ferent Times, contrary to the Peace con-
cluded between them and us, without
manifefting the leaft Willingnefs to make
us any Reparation. After the Attack, they
flaughtered ever fo many People, Men,
Women and Children; took numbers of
Prifoners; burned many Bouweries and
Plantations, and deftroyed a Quantity of
Cattle, in violation of the Article of the
Peace fpecially fought for by them,
which provided—*That in cafe any of our*
People or theirs happened to be killed, no
War fhall be waged on that account againft
each other, before and until Reparation and
Accommodation had been applied for, and
refufed. . . . . .

Thofe of *Abafiemes, Hachkinkefhacky,*
Tappan and others were alfo in this
Attack. They did our People the moft
Damage and wrought the moft cruel
Barbarity by murdering *Seven* Men and
One Woman, whom they flaughtered in
-cold Blood, in violation of their Promife

confirmed by an Oath, never taken before by them, To-wit : *May God who is above wreak Vengeance on us if we do not keep our Promise.*

Opinion of Fiscal Van Tienhoven.

PEACE having been concluded with the Natives in August *Sixteen Hundred five* and *forty*, both it and its Provisions have been infringed and broken by the Indians, as follow :

I.

By the Murder of *Fourteen* Christians in divers Places and at divers Times, between August *Sixteen Hundred five* and *forty* and the *fifteenth* of September, *Sixteen Hundred five* and *fifty*. Although demanded according to the Treaty, we have never been able to obtain Justice much less Satisfaction therefor, but on the contrary, they have paid us with Lies and false Reports, as the *Honourable* the Director-General, the Council, the Inhabitants of this Country, and our Neighbours well know.

II.

On the *Seventeenth* of laſt September, did the Indians violate and break the Treaty of Peace by force in this City of *Amſterdam*, in manner as followeth :

Firſt. Very early in the Morning, without having given any previous notice, they landed on the Shore within the Walls of this City, with *Sixty-four* Canoes and about *Five hundred* Men, all armed ; and immediately after their arrival, before ſcarcely any Burghers were afoot, a large Troop of them, in Arms, ruſhed through the Streets, and forcibly breaking open Mr. *Allerton's* Houſe, knocking the Lock off the Door, and beating the Inmates, ſearched the Premiſes by main Force, under Pretence of looking for Northern Indians. They acted in like Manner, alſo, in many Houſes within this City, until, on the Complaint of the Inhabitants and in order to prevent Mifchief, they were fhown from the *Heere Straete* (*a*) to the Shore of the *North River*, where their Canoes lay, and they had difembarked in the Morning.

The Chiefs or *Sackimaas* of the Indians, confifting of divers Nations, were invited in a friendly Manner to appear at the Council Chamber in the Fort. They did fo, and were there afked by the Members of the Council then attending, in the Prefence of the Burgomafters, Schepens and the Burgher Military Officers, the Reafon for their coming fo armed and without having given previous Notice; alfo, why they and their People committed fuch Violence and Outrage on the Burghers, breaking Locks, knocking at Doors, pufhing People and fearching Houfes, which no Dutchman could do without the Order and Authority of

(*a*) Broadway.

the Government. Therefore, the Councillors prefent and the aforefaid Burgher
Officers requefted that the Indians, for
their and our greater Security and to
prevent Mifchief and Misfortune, would
depart before Sun-down from this Ifland
to the *Nut Ifland.* This they promifed
to do, whereupon they then took their
Departure.

In ftead of keeping their Promife to
depart, there came to them in the Evening *Two Hundred* armed Indians, who,
after the fetting of the Watch, fhot
Hendrick Van Dyck, late Fifcal, with an
Arrow in his Breaft, and threatened to
fhoot *Paulus Leendertfen,* Burgher-Cap-
tain, with an Arrow. Upon thefe and
other Occurrences, the Cry arofe—
Murder! Murder! the Indians are mur-
dering the Dutch! Whereupon the
Burghers ftationed in the Fort under
Arms in order to keep good Watch, ran,
on a further Outcry, in Confufion and

without any Orders, fome through the
Gate, others over the Walls, fo that they
came into Conflict with the Indians who
were lying ready about the Shore. *Two*
Dutchmen lay killed, and *three* wounded
on the Strand, and *three* Indians were
found dead.

This Rencountre having fo come to
pafs, the Indians taking their Courfe
acrofs the River and elfewhere, burnt
many Houfes, murdered and captivated
Chriftians, killed Cattle, and after a lapfe
of fome Days ftripped *Staten Ifland* of
People and Houfes, which alfo, is in violation of the Articles of the Peace concluded Anno *Sixteen Hundred five* and
forty, whereby it was exprefsly contract-
ed, *That in cafe one or more Perfons were
killed or murdered, no General War fhall
immediately follow, but the injured Party
fhall complain to the Chiefs or Rulers of
thofe who commit the Deed, in order that
Juftice be done to the Malefactors according to Circumftances.*

Liſt of Yeomanry, Men, Women and Children, Men and Maid Servants, ſent by Baron Hendrick van de Capelle tot Ryſſel *to* New Netherland, *in the* Weſt Indies, *on* Staten Iſland, *ſince May,* 1650, *and who ſurvived that cruel and bloody Deſtruction by the Indians, in September,* 1655.

1. Capt. Andriaen Pos, with wife, five children, one ſervant, one girl; reſide yet on the Iſland.

2. Hendrik Werrinck, with wife, two children, and one ſervant; reſide on Manhattans.

3. Paul Derricks, wife, one child, and one ſervant; reſide at Fort Orange.

4. Hendrik Marcellis, wife, two children, one ſervant; reſide at Fort Orange.

5. Jan Aertſen van Heerde, with wife and eight children, reſide at Manhattans.

6. Albert Gyſbertſen van Heerde, wife,

four children, one fervant; refide at Fort Orange.

7. The wife of Arent van Hengel was married with one Severyn, now living at Manhattans. This woman hath a fon.

8. The widow of John van Oldenfeel, named Elfken, married one Mandemaker, with three children; lives on Long Ifland.

9. The widow of Jan Weffelinck, married to an Englifhman, being a carman living at the Manhattans, with three children.

. 10. Dylart, fervant of the deceafed farmer, refides at Mefpathfkill.

11. The wife of a Wheelwright, who was engaged at Zutphen, named Herminken, refides at Fort Orange, and married a Carpenter with two children.

12. Three children of corporal Gerrit Janffen van Steenwyck, tranfported hither at the Baron's expenfe.

13. Wynold, fervant of deceafed Hans Barentfen van Ofnabrugge, fent by Melyn

towards the north, has left him again, and has become an apprentice to a ſhip carpenter.

14. A boy of Barent Drieſſen van Ooſteveng, lives with a farmer on Long Iſland.

15. A child from Heenderen, called " the maimed child," reſides at Breukelen, oppoſite Manhattans.

In all 67 living ſouls. Recorded in this manner at Zutphen, on the 14th November, 1657, by the wife of Capt. Pos, and by the farmer Jan Aertſen van Heerde.

Proclamation.

Honourable, Beloved, Faithful !

IT cannot, at leaſt ought not, be un-known to, or forgotten by, any among us, that the all good and gracious God hath vouchſafed to, and beſtowed upon, this budding Province and the Inhabitants thereof, many ſpecial

Favours, Bleffings and Benefits, among the leaft of which are an increafe of Population; a Merciful Protection againft a menacing and dreaded War with our Neighbours, unexpectedly transformed into a wifhed-for and acceptable Peace; a particular augmentation of Profperity and Trade, and a bountiful and bleffed Harveft and continued Health.

As we ufed not with fufficient care, but rather ungratefully abufed thefe Favours and many other of God's Special Benefits and Bleffings, God hath been moved for our Admonition, to change his Favours towards us, vifiting and juftly chaftening, if not punifhing, us at the going out of the laft Year, by a fudden and unexpected Incurfion of the Wild Barbarous Natives of thefe Lands, by whofe cruel and murderous Hands many Inhabitants of this Province were pitileffly murdered and bereft of Property and Life; many Bouweries, Plantations

and Houfes burned, and the common
Weal fo thrown back, that we may with
juftice exclaim with the Prophet in the
Lamentations: How hath the Lord
covered us with a Cloud in his Anger
and caft down from Heaven unto the
Earth the beauty of the Land: The Lord
hath fwallowed up our Habitations and
hath not pitied; He hath cut off in His
fierce Anger our Horn; He hath drawn
back His right Hand from before the
Enemy, and He burnt as a raging Fire,
which devoureth all around us, who ftill
are fpared like a Hovel in a Cucumber
Garden, as a warning that all of us fhall
in like Manner perifh, unlefs we turn us
from our Ingratitude and heinous Sins;
we who ftill remain being Sinners no lefs
than the other Inhabitants of this Province on whom we have feen fall not the
Tower of Siloh but the Wrath of God
out of the Heavens, which through want
of Care and true Penance is ftill hanging
over our Heads.

In order then to deprecate this from the All good God, and to draw again on us, in place of His righteous Punifhment, His gracious Favours, Bleffings and Benefits, We the Director General and Council of *New Netherland*, have deemed it highly neceffary to ordain a Day of General Fafting and Prayer, which fhall be holden on the firft *Wednefday* in the Month of *March*, being the *firft* day of the faid Month; therefore we charge all our Subjects to repair in the fore and after Noon of the Day aforefaid, to the Church, or where Men are wont to hear God's Word, in order, after hearing the fame, with contrite and humble Hearts, to invoke together, with one Accord, the Name of the Lord; to Pray and Implore His Divine Majefty to be pleafed to ftay the Flood of His Wrath and the Clouds of His Anger, which began to pour down on us, and to change them into Streams of his ancient Favour and Mercy, avert-

ing all deftroying War from us and all
our good Inhabitants, or fhould His Majefty otherwife order, for the Glory of
His Name, the wider Propagation of His
Gofpel and for the Security of this Province and its Inhabitants, then that the
all Beneficent God would pleafe our
flender Might and Mean fo to blefs; to
endue the Director General and Council
together with all Inferiour Officers, People
and Subjects with Wifdom, Underftand-
ing and Fortitude, to the End that the
good Inhabitants, brought hither by his
Hand and outftretched Arm, and hitherto
protected againft the Power and Cruelty
of a Barbarous People, may be taken and
remain henceforth fheltered under His
Wings, and that fuch Means may to that
End be defigned and put in practice as
His Majefty will vouchfafe to blefs to the
greater Glory of His Name. Likewife
to pray God the Lord for continuous
Health and Profperity of Trade and

Agriculture, but chiefly for a proper and grateful Ufe of his gracious Favours and Benefits.

To the End that all this may be better, more zealoufly and more unanimoufly put in Practice, we interdict and forbid, during Divine Service, on the aforefaid Day of Fafting and Prayer, all playing of Ball and Billiards, all Hunting, Fifhing, Sailing, Plowing, Sowing, Mowing, and all unlawful Games, fuch as Dice and Intemperance, under pain of Arbitrary Correction and Punifhment, hereunto provided. In like Manner, will we have all Minifters of God's Holy Word, within our Government, admonifhed and requefted to adapt their Sermons and Prayers to the End aforefaid. Thus done and concluded in our Council holden in Fort *Amfterdam* in *New Netherland* the *twenty-feventh* January, Anno 1656.